Spooks

Published by Granada Publishing 1983
Granada Publishing Limited
8 Grafton Street, London W1X 3LA
Reprinted 1984

Text copyright © Granada Publishing
Illustrations copyright © Colin Hawkins

British Library Cataloguing in Publication Data
Hawkins, Colin
Spooks
I. Title
828′.91407   PR6058.A/

ISBN 0 246-12098-3

Printed in Italy by
New Interlitho, Milan

Spooks

By Colin and Jacqui Hawkins
and a ghost writer

GRANADA

Ghosts...

are just like you and me except that.....

..now you see
them......
and now
you don't.

Ghost Guises

Ghosts mostly appear as floppy white sheets. (They are said to materialize). Other spooks take different shapes. These are some you may – or may not – see.

Regular sheet ghosts (wraiths)

Several ghosts together are known as a shriek of ghosts.

Headless spook.

Bodiless spook

Terrifying ghost.

Terrified ghost

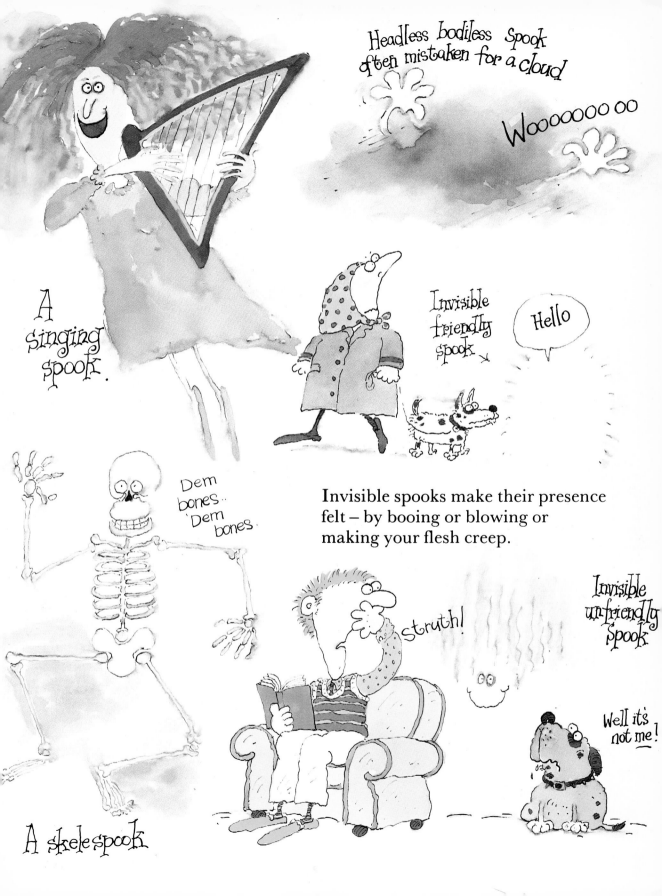

Headless bodiless Spook often mistaken for a cloud

Woooooo oo

A singing spook.

Invisible friendly spook →

Hello

Dem bones.. 'Dem bones.

Invisible spooks make their presence felt – by booing or blowing or making your flesh creep.

Struth!

Invisible unfriendly spook

Well it's not me!

A skelespook

Spook Species.

Spooks can never change. When they return from the dead to haunt the living, they come as they were in life.
Accompanied by his faithful haggis, a Scottish spook plays his ghastly pipes as he stalks the castle battlements.

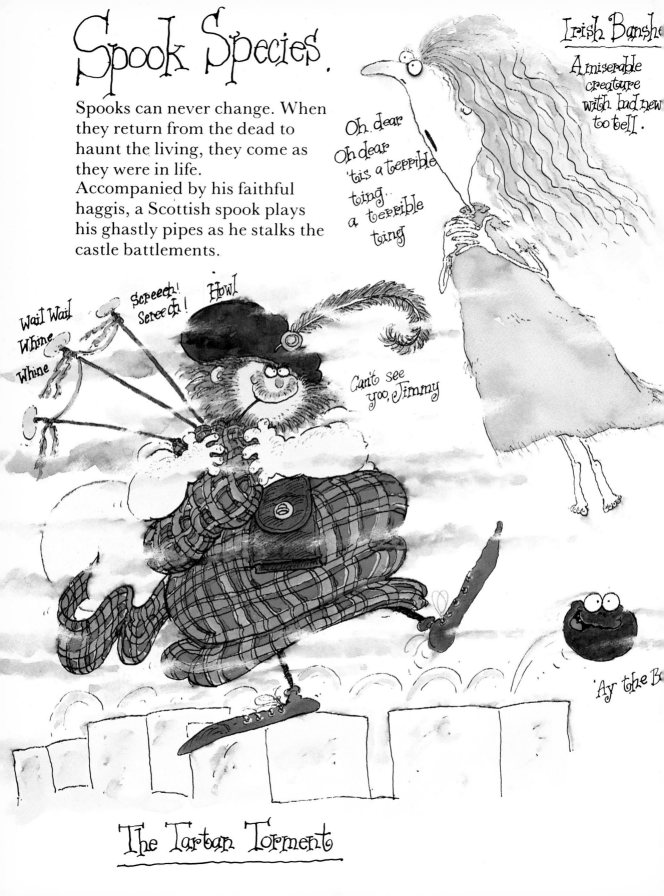

Irish Banshee

A miserable creature with bad news to tell.

Oh, dear Oh dear 'tis a terrible ting. a terrible ting

Wail Wail Whine Whine

Screech! Screech!

Howl

Can't see yoo, Jimmy

'Ay the B

The Tartan Torment

Animal Apparitions

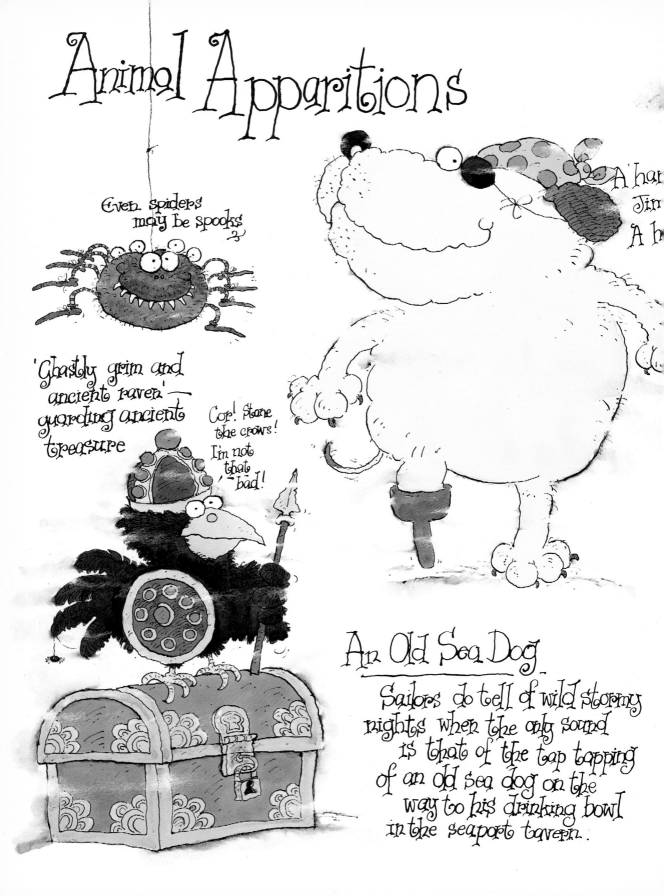

Even spiders may be spooks

'Ghastly grim and ancient raven' — guarding ancient treasure

Cor! Stone the crows! I'm not that bad!

A ha...
Jin...
A h...

An Old Sea Dog

Sailors do tell of wild stormy nights when the only sound is that of the tap tapping of an old sea dog on the way to his drinking bowl in the seaport tavern.

A spooky stroke

Hairy Scary Bear

A big Mac for me Mac'

Cats can see ghosts and be ghosts

Watch for Hair standing on end

I'm not that bad am I?

oo oooo

Even dead dogs fear ravens on their noses.

A rare monocycling bear — haunts circus rings and Macdonalds hamburger bars.

A Famous Phantom.

The Flying Dutchman

Condemned to sail the seven seas forever, the Dutchman brings death and destruction to all who witness the passing of his ship, so DON'T LOOK AT THIS PAGE

Dick Turpin, on his famous mare Black Bess, preys on those with full piggy banks at lonely zebra crossings.

The loneliest Roman of them all searches for his legion 2000 years too late.

Another Famous Phantom.

'Your piggy or your life.'

A totally unknown phantom

Quo vadis?

'or your sugar lumps'

Spook horse shoes get a lot of wear.

Spook Spotting

The lights dim, a freezing draught of air whistles under the unopened door, you hear footsteps coming towards you, nearer, nearer, nearer, the dog whines, the door handle turns and . . . you think you've seen a ghost? Don't kid yourself, it's not that easy. Spooks are no fools. You have to be really smart to spot a spook.

Most spooks are snobs, so don't bother spook spotting in high rise flats or council estates. Go to posh places where there are large old houses.

'Sit Sirrah'.

Woof!

Typical Elizabethan mansion spook with cur.

Remember: You'll never find a spook in a semi.

Heads are frequently car because of the low ceilings.

Lots of monks, nuns and vicars become ghosts. So always look in churches and convents. Nuns and monks wear flapping garments for most of their lives so they are well equipped when they die. Listen for their chilling chant as they float about the cloisters a little above the cold stone floors, telling their beads.

As well as being snobbish, spooks tend to be set in their ways – they always remain at the level they knew. This only presents problems when the floor level rises rather than falls over the centuries and we witness the phenomenon of the footless ghost.

Ghostly Habits

Mother Superior. & (floats higher than the other sisters.)

A pare of holy ghosts

Father O'Flaherty fresh from the flames of hell.

traying balls are a constant nuisance.

Transports to Terror

You are walking alone along a country road. It is dark and silent, except for the rustle of horse chestnut leaves and the thud of a falling conker. Suddenly you hear the thunder of hooves, the jangle of a harness, the creaking of coach wheels. Can this be the last bus?

Cold and tired you get out the fare, but DO NOT press your silver into the conductor's icy hand. Do not be tempted. For no-one returns from a lift in the headless coachman's carriage.

There's always room in a spook's sedan chair...

For travellers who have a life time to spare...

'Only another 1,000,000 years'

'Room for one more inside'

'Soon be my turn to sit down'

'legs worn to the bone'

Hunting the Haunting

Are you brave? Could you sit in a dark cold crypt full of scuttling spiders, with slimy things slithering across the floor and gruesome ghouls moaning and groaning and dragging their chains and creeping up behind you. If so, spook spotting is for you.

Apart from nerves and guts all you need is a pig or cat and a few essential aids.

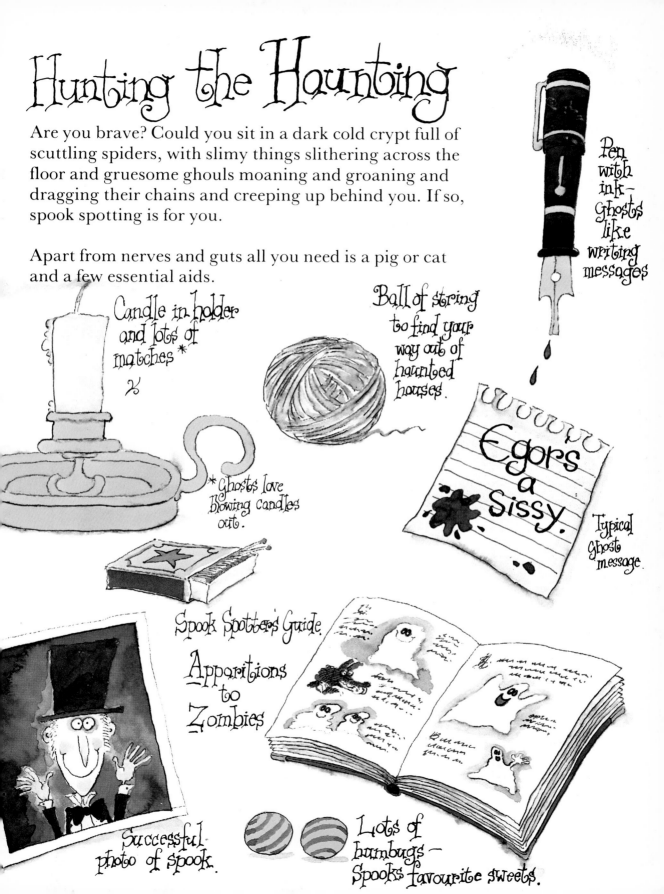

Pen with ink – Ghosts like writing messages

Candle in holder and lots of matches *

Ball of string to find your way out of haunted houses.

* Ghosts love blowing candles out.

Egors a Sissy.

Typical Ghost message.

Spook Spotter's Guide.
Apparitions to Zombies

Successful photo of spook.

Lots of humbugs – Spooks favourite sweets.

Mummy

Daddy

Mona

Bob

Hairy and Scary

The O'Gools

Ghosts never move. They haunt the places in which they lived. The O'Gools are typical. They try not to disrupt the nice people who now live in their house but every so often one of them slips up and gets seen. Screams, tears, terror – if only the living knew how harmless these ghosts are:

For a start there's Dad, Mr Fingal Drool O'Gool, once a head teacher but a shadow of his former self. Then there's Mummy, Ginny O'Gool, whose fondness for spirits is famous, the older children Ralph the Wraith and Mona the moaner, the identically ghastly twins, Float and Gloat, and the pets Hairy and Scary.

Mummy and Daddy teach the young ones how to haunt without hurting. But Ralph and Mona enjoy throwing on a sheet and shocking half the neighbourhood. It's hard to keep them home at nights. Even the pets like to pop up in unexpected places and petrify the population.

"There's a poo in the loo"
it must be you."

Float

Gloat

High Fibre Diet

At night, when the real family have gone to bed, the O'Gools materialize for breakfast. They need building up to keep fit for haunting. Like ghosts themselves, ghost food has no substance and does not comply with the law of gravity.

Nor, under the influence of the children, does the furniture. Ghosts learn to levitate when they are very young and making other objects rise into the air is the favourite game of spook children. Objects flying about a room like frisbies are usually the work of undisciplined young spooks. The O'Gools never allow their children to play such games.

Ghosti pops

Gloa Gla

Skimmed milk

hic!

Miaow!

buoyant cereal bowl.

Float's Glass

Order, Order

Dog's Breakfast

'Woof Woof'

'Breakfast each night keeps a ghost ghostie white.'

(Old ghost proverb.)

Work for Weirdos.

At midnight it is time for work. Some places have to be haunted and Mr O'Gool, for one, would never let people down. He and Hairy clock in on the stroke of twelve every night.

Shh!

Dog's Delight

Every dog has his night and tonight is mine!

The Haunting Hound.

Shh!!
Silence is essential for a successful haunting.

Mona Ralph

Daddy

Hairy really has disappeared

Ralph and Mona follow their father for a bit of fiendish fun. They practise uncanny screams and demonic laughs – but still fail to frighten anyone.

'They haven't the knack,' says their father, Fingal the Fearsome Phantom. He does not have high hopes for his children.

Hooligans a haunting

Mona and Ralph spend all night trying to distress the neighbours, ringing doorbells, tapping at windows, turning over dustbins. But it has no effect. People have grown used to things that go bump in the night. Nothing surprises them. Even the dogs and cats aren't scared of the two young ghouls. They might just as well have gone to school and learnt a bit from their elders.

A Haunting Song
Listen in the dark, listen in the dark
Cats wailing, dogs barking
Dustbins flying, doors banging
Floorboards creaking, taps dripping
Ghosts lurking, ghosts slipping
Silently through the night.

Crying
Cockles
and
mussels

A Night of Toils

With her husband gone a hauntin', Ginny is left at home to play the role of bored houseghost. Light fingered, she tinkles a rag on the grand piano while the hoover and the broom and the duster dance in appreciation. Housework is a hoot. She is a spook with a sparkle, a spectre with splendour.

Meanwhile, Dad is hard at it, nose to the tombstone. In a moment of weakness, he's left his job of haunting the school and is down in the graveyard with a crowd of disreputable, disembodied unearthly beings – his best friends.

Grave Matters

It's tomb opening at the local cemetery.

Ellie Nuisance

Sybil the Sylph

Desmond the Demon

Good health

cheers

When Dad rolls home, he kisses his wife (and misses),
tells Ralph and Mona they are too bad at haunting to
miss a single night at school, tells Float and Gloat they
are too young to disappear under his nose and upbraids
Hairy and Scary for making themselves so scarce. Then
he eats his supper and stands up, the better to tell them a
ghost story. The Pie-Eyed Piper of Hamelin is their
favourite. 'Once there was this piper . . .

. . . hypnotised by he piper,

the rats danced themselves to death but this did not stop them bopping. Their ghosts dance on for ever and ever and ever . . . . .

And at the end of the night the O'Gools say their prayers for the living and disappear. They float into a small iron box, bolt its door and wait for night to come again. If you find a locked box in your house do not try to open it.

You never know what will come out.

Good night, sleep tight.

The End

DATE DUE